MOVING WORDS
About a Flower

K. C. Hayes • Illustrated by **Barbara Chotiner**

ini Charlesbridge

One summer day rain clouds rolled
high above a gray city sidewalk.

Lightning
flashed,

and a million silver raindrops filled the sky, falling falling falling past birds and buildings and hitting the sidewalk with a **splash.**

and with it, a rainbow. And though a pot of gold, this rainbow ended right above a crack

in the sidewalk.

And while all the people hurried by in their great big boots and shoes,

a tiny sprout popped UP.

Soon that tiny sprout became a dandelion and opened its yellow petals to a world of gray concrete and CARS.

As the days passed, the yellow dandelion grew **bigger**

and **bigger,**

and
within a
few weeks,
it had become
a feathery
white ball of
seeds.

On the first day of fall, the wind began to b l o w, and the dandelion began to bend. Soon one of its seeds

took to the air.

Then another.

And another

And another

That evening
the
dandelion's
last
three

All night long

those three
little seeds

sailed on the wild wind.

In a field far away, the first seed landed in a brand-new home and then the second seed

and then the third.

Fall turned to winter.

Fat flakes of snow fell

until a thick blanket

the three little seeds

The sky turned gray.

day after day after day,

of white covered

in that faraway field.

Spring arrived.

And each of the little

The snow
melted.

dandelion seeds sent a root

into the rich brown soil.

Soon the three little dandelions had sprouted bright yellow flowers of their own. But sad to say, the first dandelion was nibbled by a deer.

The second dandelion grew a little **bigger** and a little **yellower**, but even sadder to say,

it was stepped on by a rather large moose.

But as the sun shone down and the bees *buzzed by,* the third dandelion grew **big,** and then it grew some more and opened all its **yellow petals** to a home of green grass and clover.

And a few weeks later, just as you might have expected,

the yellow dandelion had become a white ball of seeds.

When the sun came up the next day, a child wandered across that faraway field, looking for the perfect dandelion.

At last   she found it,

plucked it,

took a mighty breath . . .

and
wh o o

home.

to a
brand-new

sailed
away

sh!

The dandelion seeds

A Dandelion's Life

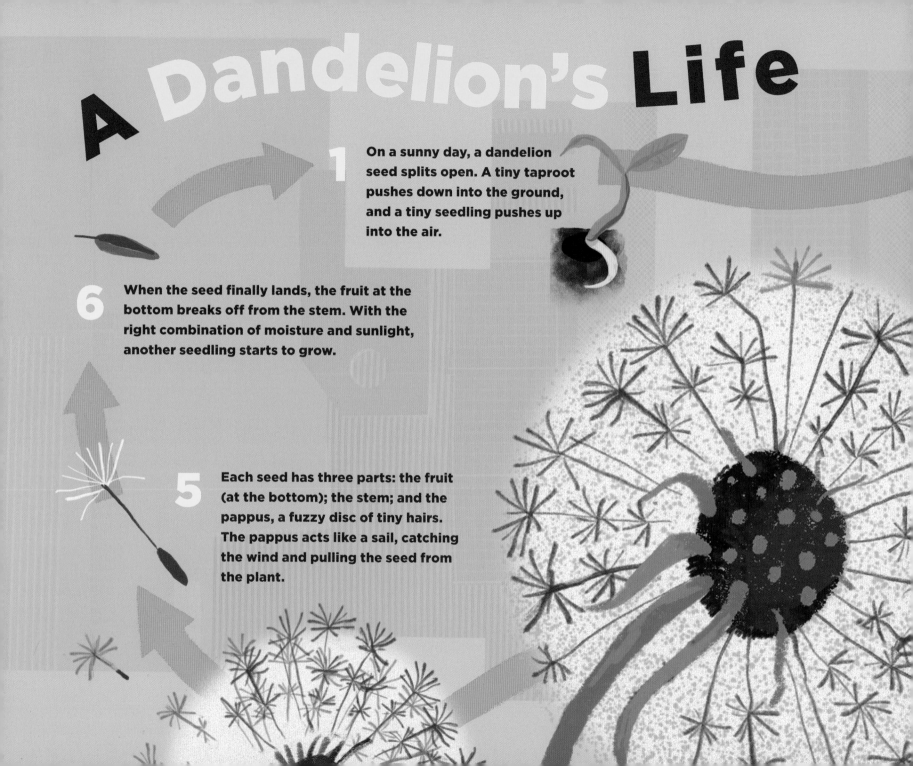

1 On a sunny day, a dandelion seed splits open. A tiny taproot pushes down into the ground, and a tiny seedling pushes up into the air.

6 When the seed finally lands, the fruit at the bottom breaks off from the stem. With the right combination of moisture and sunlight, another seedling starts to grow.

5 Each seed has three parts: the fruit (at the bottom); the stem; and the pappus, a fuzzy disc of tiny hairs. The pappus acts like a sail, catching the wind and pulling the seed from the plant.

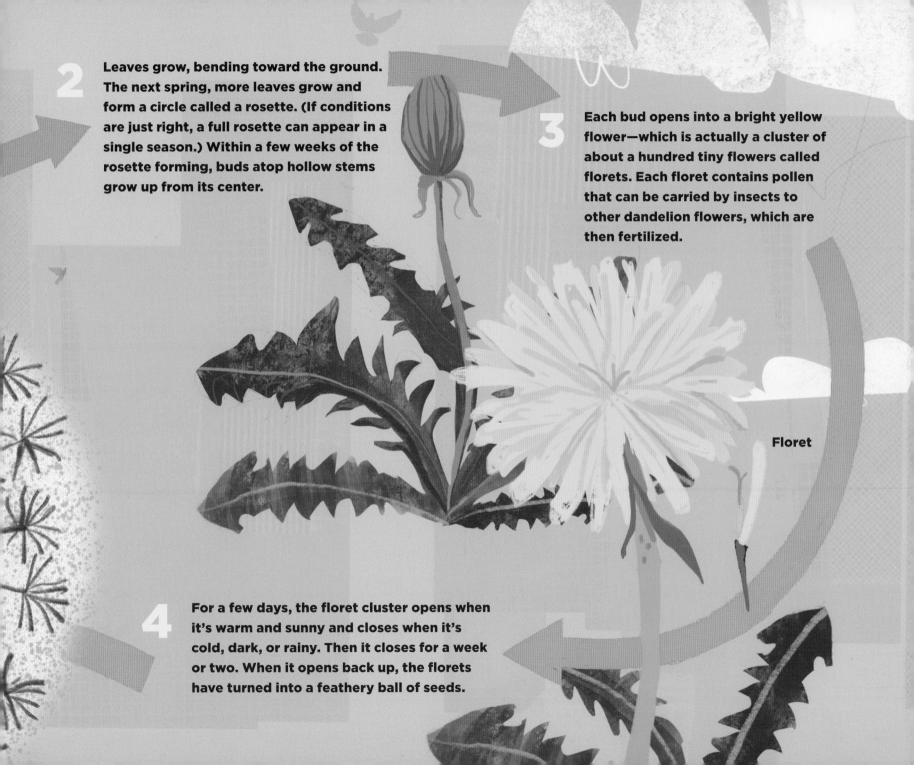

2 Leaves grow, bending toward the ground. The next spring, more leaves grow and form a circle called a rosette. (If conditions are just right, a full rosette can appear in a single season.) Within a few weeks of the rosette forming, buds atop hollow stems grow up from its center.

3 Each bud opens into a bright yellow flower—which is actually a cluster of about a hundred tiny flowers called florets. Each floret contains pollen that can be carried by insects to other dandelion flowers, which are then fertilized.

Floret

4 For a few days, the floret cluster opens when it's warm and sunny and closes when it's cold, dark, or rainy. Then it closes for a week or two. When it opens back up, the florets have turned into a feathery ball of seeds.

How Do Dandelions Fly?

Most dandelion seeds will land just six feet or so from the parent plant. But on a calm, sunny day, the wind can rise upward, which gives a few lucky seeds the chance to climb into the sky. Then they can travel a half mile or more!

Scientists have discovered two engineering tricks that help the seed stay aloft:

1. Each hair of the pappus creates a tiny swirl of air. These swirls push against one another and create drag, or air resistance.
2. As air passes between the hairs, it rotates in a circular pattern just above the pappus. This pattern, called a vortex ring, creates even more drag.

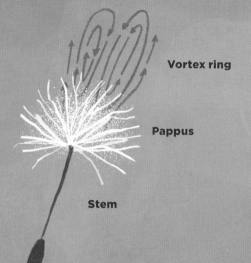

Vortex ring

Pappus

Stem

Fruit

When Do Dandelions Bloom?

In very warm areas, dandelions can bloom year-round. In temperate regions, they bloom most often in late spring, but their bright yellow flowers can appear in spring, summer, or fall. A few lucky seeds can survive the winter and grow into flowers in the spring. But most dandelions grow from taproots already in the ground.

One Tough (and Tasty) Flower

Even if their taproots are cut, dandelions can still keep growing. And they're perennials, which means they can bloom year after year. All that is why many farmers and gardeners don't like dandelions. But they're actually pretty good food: their leaves are packed with vitamins and can be eaten raw or cooked (if an adult says it's OK). They're also a tasty meal for lots of animals, from birds, rabbits, and deer to cows, pigs, and goats.

Author's Note of Thanks

I'd like to thank botanist John Pierce for his invaluable advice, suggestions, and corrections during the writing of this book.

I'd also like to make note of the sources that I found most helpful in my research:

Beal, William J. *Seed Dispersal*. Reprint of the 1898 Athenaeum Press edition, Project Gutenberg, 2008. https://www.gutenberg.org/files/26158/26158-h/26158-h.htm

Bond, W., G. Davies, and R. Turner. "The Biology and Non-Chemical Control of Dandelion (*Taraxacum* Spp.)." Coventry, UK: HDRA, Ryton Organic Gardens, October 2007. https://www.gardenorganic.org.uk/sites/www.gardenorganic.org.uk/files/organic-weeds/taraxacum-spp.pdf

Caryopsis, Johnny. "The Biology of Dandelions." NatureNorth.com. http://www.naturenorth.com/summer/dandelion/Dandelion2.html

Cummins, Cathal, et al. "A Separated Vortex Ring Underlies the Flight of the Dandelion." *Nature* 52 (2018): 414–418. https://doi.org/10.1038/s41586-018-0604-2

Hourdajian, Dara. "Dandelion (*Taraxacum officinale*)." *Introduced Species Summary Project*. Columbia University. Updated November 13, 2006. http://www.columbia.edu/itc/cerc/danoff-burg/invasion_bio/inv_spp_summ/Taraxum_officinale.htm

For Cyndy—K. C. H.

To my little inspirations, Ace and Logyn—B. C.

Published by Charlesbridge
9 Galen Street
Watertown, MA 02472
(617) 926-0329
www.charlesbridge.com

Printed in China
(hc) 10 9 8 7 6 5 4 3 2 1

Illustrations done in mixed traditional media
    and digital collage
Display and text type set in Gotham
    by Tobias Frere-Jones
Color separations and printing by 1010 Printing
    International Limited in Huizhou,
    Guangdong, China
Production supervision by Jennifer Most Delaney
Designed by Kristen Nobles and Jon Simeon

Library of Congress Cataloging-in-Publication Data
Names: Hayes, K. C. (George K. C.), author. | Chotiner, Barbara,
    illustrator.
Title: Moving words about a flower / K. C. Hayes; illustrated by
    Barbara Chotiner.
Description: Watertown, MA: Charlesbridge, 2022. | Includes
    bibliographical references. | Audience: Ages 3–7. | Audience:
    Grades K–1. | Summary: Follows the fortunes of a single dandelion,
    springing up in a crack of the sidewalk but living to spread its
    seeds to fertile ground. Includes information on the life cycle of a
    dandelion.
Identifiers: LCCN 2020052033 (print) | LCCN 2020052034 (ebook)
    | ISBN 9781623541651 (hardcover) | ISBN 9781632899613 (ebook)
Subjects: LCSH: Dandelions—Juvenile fiction. | Dandelions—Life
    cycles—Juvenile fiction. | Picture books for children. | CYAC:
    Dandelions—Fiction. | Life cycles (Biology)—Fiction. | LCGFT:
    Picture books.
Classification: LCC PZ7.1.H3962 Mo 2022 (print) | LCC PZ7.1.H3962
    (ebook) | DDC [E]—dc23
LC record available at https://lccn.loc.gov/2020052033
LC ebook record available at https://lccn.loc.gov/2020052034